For Debbie Marten
J. W.

For my Jenna
J.

First U.S. edition 2016

Library of Congress Catalog Card Number pending
ISBN 978-0-7636-8944-5

16 17 18 19 20 21 FGF 10 9 8 7 6 5 4 3 2 1

Printed in Shenzhen, Guangdong, China

This book was typeset in IM FELL Double Pica.
The illustrations were created digitally.

Nosy Crow
an imprint of
Candlewick Press
99 Dover Street
Somerville, Massachusetts 02144

www.nosycrow.com
www.candlewick.com

# PoLES APaRT

Jeanne Willis

illustrated by Jarvis

nosy crow

An imprint of Candlewick Press

As everyone knows,
penguins are found at the South Pole
and never at the North Pole.

At least, not until the day . . .

the Pilchard-Browns got lost on their way to a picnic.
Mr. Pilchard-Brown was in charge of the map.
He told everyone to turn **right** at the snowman.
Which was **wrong**.

Now here they all were, on the other side
of the world — Mr. and Mrs. Pilchard-Brown,
Peeky, Poots, and Pog —

drifting toward an **enormous,** furry white . . .

# something.

"Is it a lion? Is it a tiger?" asked Peeky and Poots.

"Is it a picnic blanket?" asked Pog.

The enormous something looked them up and down.

He had never seen anything like the Pilchard-Browns before.

"I'm Mr. White," he said.

"I'm a polar bear, and you are?"

"Parrots!" said Peeky and Poots.

"Pork pies!" said Pog.

"We're penguins," said Mrs. Pilchard-Brown.

"What are you doing here?" wondered Mr. White.

"We're going to a picnic at the South Pole," said Pog.

"This is the **North Pole,** my friends," said Mr. White.

"The South Pole is **12,430** miles *that* way."

"Anyone can make a mistake,"
Mr. Pilchard-Brown said with a shrug.

"Don't think of it as a mistake," said Mr. White.
"Think of it as the start of a big adventure.
Maybe I could help you find your way home.
I have often dreamed of being the first
polar bear to reach the South Pole."

"Mom says we should always follow our dreams," said Peeky.
"Dad says we should always follow him," said Poots.
"Lead the way, Mr. White," said Mrs. Pilchard-Brown.

The penguins followed Mr. White over land and sea.

"Eek!" said Peeky.

"Whoa!" said Poots.

"Can we have our picnic now?" asked Pog.
But it wasn't the best spot,
so they followed Mr. White
all the way to . . .

the United States.

"Howdy!" said Mr. Pilchard-Brown.

"Busy!" said Peeky.

"Buzzing!" said Poots.

"Can we have our picnic now?" asked Pog.
"Not yet, dear," said Mrs. Pilchard-Brown.

The U.S. was **awesome,**
but it wasn't home, so they followed
Mr. White all the way to . . .

England.

"How do you do?" said Mr. Pilchard-Brown.

"Gray!" said Peeky.

"Grand!" said Poots.

"Now can we have our picnic?" asked Pog.
"Not here, dear," said Mrs. Pilchard-Brown.
England was **charming,** but it wasn't home,
so they followed Mr. White all the way to . . .

# Italy.

"*Ciao!*" said Mr. Pilchard-Brown.

"Wet!" said Peeky.

"Wonderful!" said Poots.

"I need to pee," said Pog.
"Not here, dear,"
said Mrs. Pilchard-Brown.

Italy was *magnifico,* but it wasn't home,
so they followed Mr. White all the way to . . .

India.

"*Namaste!*"
said Mr. Pilchard-Brown.

"Hot!" said Peeky.

"Huge!" said Poots.

"Put the python down, dear,"
said Mrs. Pilchard-Brown.

India was dazzling,
but it wasn't home, so
they followed Mr. White
all the way to . . .

# Australia.

"G'day!" said Mr. Pilchard-Brown.

"Faster!" said Peeky.

"Fun!" said Poots.

"Can we have our picnic *now*?" asked Pog.

"Soon," said Mrs. Pilchard-Brown.

Australia was **bonzer,** but it still wasn't home,

so they followed Mr. White . . .

over the land and over the sea.
On and on they went.

"Are we almost there?"
    asked Peeky, Poots, and Pog.

"It's not far now," said Mr. White,

and they followed him left, right,

left, right,

all the way . . .

# home!

"**Please stay, Mr. White,**" said Peeky and Poots.

"You can share our picnic," said Pog.

But the South Pole wasn't his home.
He was a **polar bear,**
and polar bears live at the North Pole.

Which is why he said good-bye and
traveled **12,430** miles, all the way back to . . .

the North Pole,

where he belonged.

He'd followed his **wildest** dream and had
the **best** adventure. He was happy to be home but sad
that he would **never** see a penguin again.

But then, to Mr. White's delight . . .

# he did!

"Hello. How did you get here?" he said.

Then he heard a familiar voice.
"Someone put **my egg** in your hat,"
said Mrs. Pilchard-Brown.
"Can we have our picnic *now*?" asked Pog.
"Please make yourselves at home!" said
   Mr. White.

And they did. Because even though penguins
   and polar bears lives poles apart, **friends**
       are always welcome.